Weekly Reader Presents

Fraggle Countdown

By Michaela Muntean

Pictures by Diane Dawson Hearn

Muppet Press
Holt, Rinehart and Winston
NEW YORK

Published by Holt, Rinehart and Winston,
383 Madison Avenue, New York, New York 10017.

Library of Congress Cataloging in Publication Data
Muntean, Michaela.
Fraggle countdown.
Summary: Fifteen Fraggles set off on a day of
adventures at the end of which Wembley finds he has been
left all alone.
1. Children's stories, American. [1. Stories in
rhyme. 2. Puppets—Fiction. 3. Counting] I. Hearn,
Diane Dawson, ill. II. Title.
PZ8.3.M89Fr 1985 [E] 84-19107

ISBN: 0-03-003264-4
First Edition

Printed in the United States of America
1 3 5 7 9 10 8 6 4 2

ISBN 0-03-003264-4

Fraggle Countdown

15 Fraggles frolic
Up, down, and in between.
One skids on a slippery rock,
And then there are

14 Fraggles playing
Loop-the-loop and skip-the-bean.
One swings on a swoople vine,
And then there are

13 Fraggles dancing
The Whirlish Derving Delve.
One trips on a wompus root,
And then there are

12 Fraggles counting
radishes one through seven.
One goes off to gather more,
And then there are

11 Fraggles leaping
Past the Gagtoothed Groan's dark den.
One gets scared and scampers home
And then there are

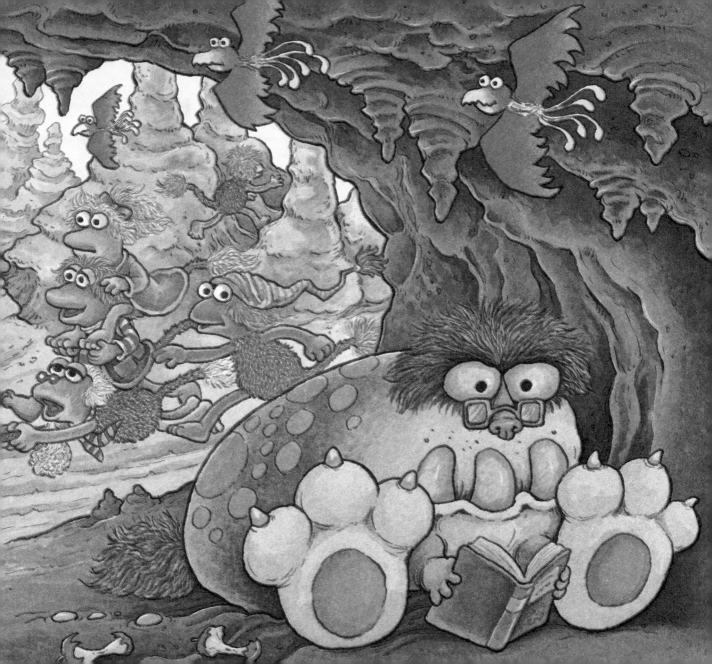

10 Fraggles jumping
Jump rope in a line.
One skips off in purple socks,
And then there are

9 Fraggles shouting,
"LET'S SING AND CELEBRATE!"
One climbs in a quiet cove,
And then there are

8 Fraggles inching
Through the Creepy Crawling Crevin.
One gets tangled in a vine
And then there are

7 Fraggles crunching
Bunches of Doozer sticks.
One says he has munched too much,
And then there are

6 Fraggles doing
A daring high-rock dive.
One looks down and turns around,
And then there are

5 Fraggles bouncing
In the cave of the Bog-Bounce Floor.
One flies high and cries, "Good-bye!"
And then there are

4 Fraggles climbing
A twisted toe-stub tree.
One of the branches breaks in two,
And then there are

3 Fraggles doing
Things Fraggles love to do.
One feels like doing nothing,
And then there are

2 Fraggles juggling
Pretty pickles just for fun.
One goes off exploring caves,
And then there is

1 Fraggle wondering
Where everyone else could be . . .
"Hey!" cries that Fraggle.
"Everyone wait for me!"